Ghost
© 2013 by Sarah Tourjee

First edition 2013.
Printed in the USA.

ISBN: 978-1-939781-02-4

Cover designed and painted by Erica Mena.
Designed and typeset by Sarah Seldomridge.

This book is available as an ebook & audiobook from Anomalous Press.

www.anomalouspress.org/books/ghost.php

ACKNOWLEDGEMENTS

I'm very grateful to my parents, my brother, my sister, my grandmothers, my friends and family (old and new), and so many people I love who reveal yourselves to be near regardless of distance, time, or circumstance. All of you have made my world so unlike the world of this short book.

I'd like to thank the Literary Arts Department at Brown University. I'd like to thank Carole Maso.

I'd finally like to thank Anomalous Press for having a vision that includes me.

GHOST

I am one voice one voice one voice one ghost. I am the disconnect, the absence. I am what's left. This is not an afterlife, but just after— this is breath that leaves a mouth and circulates into air, not the identity of the thing it has left, but merely a mist that remembers. Not vanished but not present, just an ever decreasing amount of gas. This is what I am and this is why I combine. With enough I may be enough to be something.

Is it to me to do the seeing for all the blindness that surrounds? The house teems with life, but who among these creatures sees me? I am breathed in with a snore, released with the lungs' hot air. Does the animal know the difference? Again I approach, slide under an eye, keep going. This is a brain, hot and pulsing. Within it reel the images of dreams no doubt, and I wonder will I appear there? In my life, when I was a part of something living, I wondered what this fragile organ could look like, what its mechanisms specifically entailed. People are told only metaphors—electricity is what the brain is like, or a soup carefully balanced in measurement. What you feel when you are sad, psychotic, immobile—this is not anything but misbalance, an over-salted soup. Yet now it is me, the ghost, who stirs up the soup as I pass through.

It is not my intent to drive anyone mad, but merely to cause an effect. How else can I confirm that I exist? I inhabit this house but it's these others who live here. This human and these animals. It's these bodies I've become familiar with, it's their energy that draws me in and obsesses me. When a living being contained me, I remember the necessary organ—the brain—was faulty, was stained white in the hospital's images. My body teetered, shook, and the brain forgot. I longed to visit my brain and look on it, to scrape the white patches off and allow the currents to travel uninhibited, so that then the body may have walked and the hands could lie still.

Now I am only slightly greater than air—an absence that perceives. That brain I speak of has long since decayed in the dirt. Yet still I am possessed by its phantom. I wonder if perhaps, I am its phantom? I can see what these living creatures can't. I can see them, can see myself. I can enter them, can enter the parts of them that allow them to live. Do they know it? They fill the house with their bodies, perhaps so that what's living will outnumber what's not.

Before the decay, I went to pay my respects. I traveled through the porous earth, the seams of the casket, and through the stitching of one nostril in my dead face. I floated there in the pickling of my brain's embalmment. There was nothing left to see.

Now I jump from human to dog to dog to dog to dog to dog and on and on. HELLO I am screaming, hoping that one of them will feel at least a prickling on their skin from the chaos of my energy upon them. Once there was one who heard, felt, saw me. He saw more of me than there was to see, his eyes and ears filled in the many gaps. He was mine. A gift. Proof that I existed. I could not help myself from revisiting the evidence again and again until it was he who began to fade. Ears, I enter ears I enter ears I enter ears I entered his ear I am a ghost. I entered his ear and he folded it down to lock me in. I obliged, I stayed put.

HUMAN

The drought has killed most plant life here. Brown grass tries feebly to grow in patches of yard. Dirt takes over, coating shoes, feet, fur, sidewalks. The house, one floor with only a half level basement, sits mostly on the ground provoking the entrance of insects and small animals, though little attempts to enter now that the dogs have overtaken the place.

In the area surrounding it patches of bushes or tall yellow grass reveal the occasional bloody scene, but bloody scenes are a contingency of life. Is it worth making a fuss over if you're not dead? A drought will end, but a dog attack, any attack, is never out of the question. I carry food on me, and so the dogs follow me home. I like to be prepared, I tell myself, but really, I like to be followed. Now that he is gone, I am alone except for the dogs, always.

Alone—but, there, in the corner, I squint and try to see it, the ghost.

Years ago I ran, and when I ran I ran at night. Was I chased? I ran as though he was on my heels. I heard my brother's feet behind me, his snarling and spit. Like the dream I have where I run and run because whatever chases me means to kill me, it seemed as fast as I ran it would not be fast enough. I turned to gauge my chances. The darkness spread out uninterrupted behind me. I was alone. The spit was my own. "He's not there," I said, into the dark.

When I returned he was gone. I put his things out in the yard hoping to lure him back. All night I hear the sounds of animals, the screams of mating dogs. All these years later he still hasn't returned. Now I've come full circle. I'm hunting for him, because family is family, all you've got more or less, and he was my brother.

It was me against the ghost, I think it always was. "Choose me," I kept asking him, begging, but his attention was always elsewhere. It occurred to me that I was merely alive. My messages were few, they were just small callings in the dark for reassurance. How long could I expect a person to receive them? It was the ghost, I imagined, who had real things to say, who could speak to him and give him something he could keep. I was not surprised when he left me for it. I hoped the ghost would not desert me with him, that it would stay to bridge us wherever he was. I call out for it now, but I am not answered, and if this is a bridge it is loose leafed, compromised.

DOG

We starve, dry out, cook. We live in debris, in bushes, in abandoned houses. We hunt, and finding nothing, we split our gums on the bones of our friends. We hope our thin bodies will satiate the pack. We come to the house, waiting for death, and then a miracle. We are alone, and then our leader finds us.

We owe her our lives now, our protection. There is nothing that can live alone. Hundreds are not enough to survive without her, our leader. Now we are full, and when she touches us there is calm. Now she searches, and so we search.

Yet there, something else—

At night, we sleep. But then I wake, startle, a noise, a sense. What's there? What's on us? There is nothing there, my pack doesn't stir, and yet I feel it—something foreign within my companion. He sleeps, undisturbed but now unfamiliar. I bite his ear. He wakes, annoyed, snarls. He is the same. Our leader sleeps.

GHOST

This world is desert, dry dust and things that crackle and break. This world is heat that kills anything that does not adapt or stay inside. This house is a shelter, a container to be filled. This world contains desert which contains a house which contains bodies containing bodies containing organs, brains, spirits. This house is full of ghosts, but we are not contained by walls or heat or skin. I was human when a body enclosed me, and I was stuck there within it, attached to it and forced to be it. I was physical, a shelter that crackled and broke. And now I am nothing but a current of air.

Human, hello. What are you looking for? I can see it's not me you are trying to find. When I enter your skull and fit myself between lobes I am listening intently hoping to hear it, whatever buzzes inside. I hope to catch a glimpse of what it is that you seek. What was common between us is lost now. There is no language—mutual sound—that exists between bodies and ghosts, but only rarely the fleeting sense that we've touched.

Human walks into the house with an ever increasing number of dogs following behind her. Dogs chew at woodwork, dig at the floor, sleep. Human and dogs look right at me, then turn and leave the room. Did they see me? I approach the face of one, graze its skin, settle on the bridge of a nose. I am unnoticed.

Unrest this is unrest this is a well of unrest. This is what exists in the negative space. After life comes an absence of life which is no definition at all. I can tell you what I am not, but there are no words for what I am. An absence of language exists in the area that is me, and yet there are words to say. Are they speaking?

Do they speak? Dog stares at human stares at dog stares at ghost stares at human turns away. Each species is alone in a well of itself.

HUMAN

I take the dogs for long walks around the city. We look for him, for a sign. More and more join us, appealed by the comfort of our expanding, moving mass. We walk for hours, howling and picking at dead things and dirt. "A good dog is a tired dog," I remember being told, and so we follow the railroad tracks for an hour before turning around to come back. When a fight breaks out I watch them divvy up the ranks between them. One lags behind limping, and so I pick him up to give him a rest, but even the pregnant dogs walk faster than I do.

Everyday our search widens in the same narrow directions. We inspect bridges, ledges, we travel circumference of the thickest tree trunks. We make it ten miles one day to the reservoir. Why we've chose this as our destination is anyone's guess. Dogs are not allowed in, but there are so many now, and so rules mean less and less.

I can hardly remember now where these creatures began. I have the sense they've always been with me but can this be true? At times I feel more them than me, more animal than human. They grow in number everyday and I sleep in the middle of the pack, warmed by their bodies and lulled by the tremor of breathing. I tell myself, if there were ghosts here, the dogs would surely know it—I would surely know it. They would bark and growl, I would feel on my neck that primal sense. Instead they sleep soundly, one laps at my foot, and what I experience is peace.

At one time we had a mother. Once I rubbed her legs from ankle to knee. She smiled, said "Thank you, you are kind." I was a stranger then, offering an unexpected, intimate gesture.

It was my brother who saw them—the ghosts—could not stop seeing them, and I awaken in the mornings knowing that at one time they were here.

So much went unsaid between us that now I wonder if we were both living the same reality. How would we have known? Was it so hot where he was? Were we all alone where he was? Was it the ghost he had to get away from or was it me? We collided briefly and then ricocheted away. Our voices dimmed in the distance.

DOG

Now forest, now concrete, now we are running. There are a lot of us, this is better than few. This better than starving and hiding and not knowing. Now we call out, we find more and more of ourselves, because this makes it safer and we need to be safe, and we need to not be alone. What does it mean to walk on two legs or run? This is impossible, this is a fantastic feat. She does this, and she produces food from thin air while we've scavenged for rot. She reaches out to touch us and suddenly there is calm.

We recruit now, we breed for her. We grow in numbers. We run. We spread out in all directions to clear the path as she walks. We attack anything that doesn't turn the other way.

She doesn't even know we do this for her. She walks peacefully and we try to keep it that way. She is hunting for something, and we will help her find it.

Now a trespasser, now it kicks. Now we attack. There is blood in our mouths and this could be food, but this is not food. This is an enemy and if it should be eaten she will be the one to enjoy the meal, not us. She will be pleased, we hope, but we should not get distracted. We should not let down our guard lest it get away. It yells, cries, does not understand that this is our job now. We leave the intruder in the tall grass it came out of and then run back to greet our leader as she walks.

HUMAN

One of my brother's ears folded over in a flap. He had held it that way for so long trying to block out or hold in the voices of ghosts, that the cartilage permanently creased. I remember him sometimes looking like one of the dogs, staring at some invisible thing just above me, one ear erect while the other drooped. Are these things genetic, or do ghosts choose certain sorts of people to show themselves to? It was sometimes called a gift, proof that he was protected and that by proximity so was I.

"You're there," I would say into the night, and he would answer, "You're there." Whatever else there was there was this—this echo repeating our presence back to us. Now I wake up and if I bother to say it, if I am brave enough to say it, there is only silence in response. A dog may look up at me, the wind may alert itself, but there is no voice to confirm me, there is nothing that speaks.

What was between us, what was fraught, was taken by the ghost. And this was all there was, I realize. We were each other's accounting. I existed because he saw me, and we existed together because we saw the same surrounding. But the ghost was there for him only and its presence was a rewriting. To him this desert became ghost before sand, and so we could not both live there with certainty, could not know as before that when one was there the other was or was not.

One night he looked and saw only ghost. He ran away from me, away from the house, I followed him. I was not fast enough, and at some point the sounds of our feet were inverted, at some point it was me who was pursued. How long did we run?

Or did I imagine the sounds of his feet? Was it just the dogs that followed?

We could have been going anywhere that night. We could have been going to the same place. But we did not arrive there, and he never came back. When I returned there was no one to confirm my arrival, but the dogs started showing up dying and so I brought them all in.

Now there is only one thing that could know him, there is only the ghost. And so I watch the dogs and wait for their eyes to move together to some spot on the wall, I wait for their fur to stand on end. I am older now than he was then, and we are hundreds it seems, spilling from the house, searching, crossing highways with intent.

GHOST

This plain, all this space. I am without body, identity, mind. What exists? I want to tell you that a body is what makes you, that a brain is a thing that contains you. Can air be alone can it be lonely or act or comfort or menace even kill can I be seen?

He was an exception, a fluke. What was it and how, when I entered a room, did he know it? There is nothing of me to see, I am vapor or less. Yet, he looked right at me, not away like the others. I went into his ear, dug into his brain, I needed to see what was different. He felt me, could he hear? He folded his ear over my entrance, as though that could keep me, or coax me to leave this enclosure, this new home that knew I was in it. I didn't know if he meant to keep or shoo me but how could I leave?

I can't relate to this human, even the dogs know something I don't. I don't remember being alive, only the feeling of humanity leaving me, not all at once but slowly. Was I very old? Mobility decreased and then the mind, the most human of parts, became undependable. I could not say what I already knew when it was required that I say it. And those humans I knew became diluted as well. Their names and then faces washed away. Now what was human is long gone, now I enter the faces of dogs while they sleep, and try, with my prodding, to wake them.

HUMAN

I can live here. I can live here just fine. "If I am ever lost," I tell the dogs, "start at the house and search in circles that widen." This is how we try to find him. "Understand," I say, "right." This one dog is so funny, we laugh quite a lot, and I place my palm over its shoulders and it rests and I rest. But one night I find it crawled atop another dog, tail pushed to the side. I approach them and both snarl but will not detach. I bang some pots together and they finally run out of the house. The dog comes back eventually but I am wary of it now. I avoid it.

Everywhere it seems, under tables, in closets, at the foot of my bed, puppies are appearing from the bodies of dogs. This makes me wonder what will one day appear from my own body, or if inversely things will only disappear inside it, eventually enclosing itself, enclosing me. The latter thought is startling. There sure are a lot of them now, I think as I watch the dogs multiply. Have I only just realized it? I go to the bathroom for some towels.

Their numbers make me think, if I died would these dogs eat me? If they were starving would they attack? I am sure that they would eat me, but if I were starving perhaps I'd do the same. They came to me for food, but now in their strength they bring me so much. The carcasses cover the yard. And I am comforted when I see it, this evidence that they are as determined as I am to avoid the consequences of our hunger.

I kneel down and put my arms around one of the dogs. It licks my face. I block it with my hand and it licks my hand. I am wearing my brother's shirt. I pull the dog's head to my chest. "Do you smell him?" I say to the dog.

"Do you know where he is?" The dog growls, backs away. The look in its eyes is one I have seen before. It's a look that does not know me. I stare into the dog's face and say, "Is he dead?"

When I leave I hide behind a tree until the dogs lose interest in me, move away, then I'm off. I run.

DOG

We hunt. We are deadly. We gather birds, rabbits, squirrels, possums, cats, and stragglers from intruding packs. We drag the bodies back to our den, leave the kill in the yard for our leader. She is pleased, she lets us eat. She tends to our young, cleans our wounds, provides shelter from the night. We protect her. We circle.

Our leader rubs her face to mine, scratches my neck, lets me lick. But now something comes between us, something hides her. Where mouth should be and eyes, something covers, attacks. I growl, bark, frighten it away.

Now it pulls me, tightens, attacks from within, then is gone. So is she. We will find it. We will kill any threat. We move in circles that widen, we cover all ground. We will empty this world out for her. We will be all that's left.

GHOST

The human thinks she is alone, does not know she takes me with her. She runs, then walks—how long has it been?—and now she stops. In front of us, another house, darkness, dim lights within. A knocking, she knocks. An unfamiliar body appears at the door.

They touch their hands together. I travel from one to the other, keep going and move into the house. The place is empty of dogs of humans—just one human here, and now two, plus a ghost. Where are we? Who is this? Do they speak? Not for long. Their faces press together, then bodies, hands pull, shed layers, and I enter them, let their tongues pass me from one mouth to the other. They fall to the floor.

Their bodies connect in a variety of ways—legs hooked, hands on faces, on torsos, mouths take what can be taken. I move deeper into the body. I watch from within as they enter each other, contain each other and are contained. When one presses inward, the other gives way to the push. This is the effect I long to cause and so I make myself static, imagine myself physical, a part of the act.

Their bodies, and I with them, rock on the floor slowly then faster and their insides vocal chords vibrate muscles tighten relax tighten tighten. One exits the other and I emerge as well into the air of the house. Now they slide over each other, stick to each other, and I am between them filling the microscopic spaces that remain. They quake, bodies harden, fingers clench, torsos curl, then release, fall back again to the floor.

This is not breeding like dogs multiplying, but something else. And I remember it, this fucking, a benefit of bodies of being human.

HUMAN

A consequence of bodies, as the dogs seem to know, is more bodies, and I place my hand over my stomach and imagine something lives there, something grows. Yet I know. A body is not among the things that can be given when we reach into each other and empty our hands. Still, I try. I reach into a person and try to recreate him. Other than the things he left, he no longer exists, and so I can put him wherever I wish. But the wish does not make him appear, it just changes his shape. Am I looking for remnants, or something that's whole? Would I recognize it?

I place my brother with dogs, with ghosts, with all things that can see what I can't. Why am I left out? Why am I left? "Ghost, possess me if you exist," I whisper, but I feel nothing. Nothing comes. And the dogs pace, attend to each other, to their families that grow while mine shrinks. Am I forgotten in the desert, am I lost with what's been left?

"You're there?" I say, but he is not and I know he won't be found. I know I won't be haunted. The worst of all my offenses was that I did not even know when he was upon me, if he ever was upon me.

GHOST

I visit him, the human, one who heard me, old friend, old home. But. Wind blows freely through his jaw and empty eye sockets now, and I travel with the current over the smooth edges of his skull. The rest of him is scattered, carried off by animals. Like me he is dead, but he is not a ghost.

Free from the enclosure of living in a body, is this freedom or am I lost? To exist I must be seen to be seen I must be more than nothing more than thoughts and perception I must be physical with edges to show clearly where I begin where I end just how much space I take up and what I am. What I am is only space, not a limit of it great or small, but just a field where things exist. Rocks exist there, dogs exist there, even bones.

The human who remains does not see me and yet there is something that makes me stay in that house with her. I can't call to her, I can't inhabit. We are parallel, separate, estranged. We keep moving laterally, at times the dogs may intersect.

Settled inside the skull now, I want to know, if I am where a brain should be, does this make me a brain? Is he alive if something inside his skull thinks? If the spirit is all that remains of one, and these bones are all that remain of another, can we combine to make something that lives?

There is something that keeps me from leaving this desert, leaving the house, leaving her, and looking for someone else who might hear. (I try to lift the skull from within it but as I rise I rise through it. I look down and the skull remains in the dirt.) She empties something within the walls of the house, perhaps something I can collect, like answers to questions. What is the secret of these creatures that live? How do they stay inside? How do they move the body? Or maybe it's simply the remnants of a calling out, of a search that is familiar, of an echo that compels me to stay.

The fourth book in the **Anomalous Press** series, this book was typeset and designed by Sarah Seldomridge in a limited edition of 200 copies.

Anomalous Press is dedicated to the diffusion of writing in the forms it can take. We're searching for imaginary solutions in this exceptional universe. We're thinking about you and that thing you wrote one time and how you showed it to us and we blushed.

www.anomalouspress.org

Available from **Anomalous Press**:

An Introduction to Venantius Fortunatus for Schoolchildren or Understanding the Medieval Concept World through Metonymy
by Mike Schorsch

The Continuing Adventures of Alice Spider
by Janis Freegard

Ghost by Sarah Tourjee

The Everyday Maths by Liat Berdugo
selected by Cole Swensen

Mystérieuse by Éric Suchère,
translated by Sandra Doller
selected by Christian Hawkey

Smedley's Secret Guide to World Literature
by Jonathan Levy Wainwright, IV, age 15
by Askold Melnyczuk

Sarah Tourjee's fiction has appeared in *Conjunctions, PANK, The Collagist, Wigleaf, Everyday Genius, Anomalous* and elsewhere. She is a recipient of the John Hawkes fiction prize and an &NOW award for innovative writing. She earned her MFA from Brown University and lives in Northampton Massachusetts.